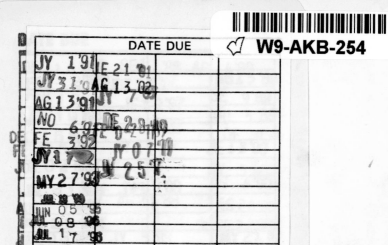

DATE DUE			
JY 1'91	IE 21 01		
JY 31'91	AG 13'02		
AG 13'91	JY 70		
NO 6'91	DE 28'09		
FE 3'92	0 28 10		
JY 17'92	JY 07 10		
MY 27'93	Y 25 T		
JU 18'93			
JUN 05 '95			
JUL 08 '96			
JUL 17 '98			
JUL 23 '98			
SE 16'00			

201-9500   PRINTED IN U.S.A.

E
Br

Broekel, Ray
The mystery of the stolen base

EAU CLAIRE DISTRICT LIBRARY

THE MYSTERY OF THE STOLEN BASE

THE MYSTERY OF
THE STOLEN BASE

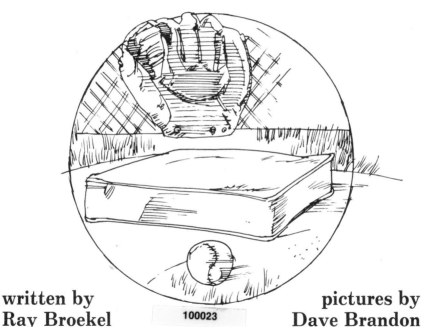

written by
Ray Broekel

100023

pictures by
Dave Brandon

CAROLRHODA BOOKS

MINNEAPOLIS, MINNESOTA U.S.A.

EAU CLAIRE DISTRICT LIBRARY

Copyright © 1980 by CAROLRHODA BOOKS, INC.

All rights reserved. International copyright secured.
Manufactured in the United States of America.

International Standard Book Number: 0-87614-111-4
Library of Congress Catalog Card Number: 79-52405

1 2 3 4 5 6 7 8 9 10 85 84 83 82 81 80

"Come on, Mark! Hit the ball!" Dave Weisman shouted.

Mark Murphy was at bat for the Tigers. It was the last inning. The Tigers were one run behind the Robins. There were two outs. Liz Harris was on third.

"It's up to you!" Mark heard Mrs. Zervas shout. She was one of the player's grandmother. She was also the Tigers' biggest fan. "Drive Liz in! Get a hit!"

Other fans were yelling too. "Come on, Mark!" "Win the game for us!"

Mark dug in at the plate. He got a good hold on the bat. The pitcher threw a fast one. Mark took a swing. He missed.

"Strike one," the umpire called.

The Robin fans cheered. The Tiger fans were quiet.

The next pitch was a ball. So was the next.

"Come on, Mark! Do your thing!" Mark heard Mrs. Zervas again.

He felt lucky about the next pitch. "This is the one," he told himself. "I'm going to hit this one right out of the park."

The pitch came. Mark swung. He had a hit. The ball sailed over the left fielder's head. It was over the fence! A home run!

The Tigers began to cheer. The fans were cheering too.

"We won! We won!" shouted Dave.

Mark was rounding the bases. He was crossing second when it happened. His shoe caught in a rip in the corner of the base. Mark fell to the ground. He grabbed his foot.

Coach Peterson ran out on the field. "What is it, Mark?"

"My ankle," Mark said. "It's my ankle."

"Let me see," said the coach. "Hmm. No broken bones. You're lucky, Mark. You have just twisted your ankle." Coach Peterson helped Mark to his feet. "Take a step," he said. "But take it easy."

Mark took a careful step. "Man, does it ever hurt," he said. Then he limped around third and across home plate to make the home run legal.

"Great hit, Mark," said Dave. He helped Mark to the bench. The Tigers crowded around. Many of the fans had come down from the stands too. One of them was Mrs. Zervas.

"Good work, Mark," she said. "How's your foot?"

"It hurts," Mark told her. "But it will be fine in time for Friday's game."

Then Coach Peterson said, "Let's all go to Werner's Ice Cream Shop. It's on me."

"Anything we want, Coach?" Liz asked.

"The way you eat?" said Dave. "Do you think the coach is nuts?"

Everyone laughed.

There was practice the next morning.
Mark still limped a little. He was just going
to watch. He walked to the park. But when
he got there, the team wasn't practicing.
They were hunting for something.

"What's going on, Liz?" he asked.

"You won't believe this," she said. "Somebody stole second base."

Mark laughed. "Pretty funny, Liz," he said.

"Really, Mark," said Liz. "Somebody really did steal second base."

"Who would want it?" Mark asked. "Second base is why I'm limping."

"Got me," Liz said. "But second base is gone. We've looked all over the park."

"How about that big dog that's always around?" Mark said. "It carries off balls and things all the time. Maybe it stole the base. It's probably lying somewhere under a bush."

EAU CLAIRE DISTRICT LIBRARY

"We already looked under all the bushes," said Liz. "We've looked all over. But no base."

"So what are we doing for practice?" Mark asked.

"Coach Peterson is getting a piece of cardboard," said Liz.

"What about the big game on Friday?"

"We'll have to buy a new one," Liz said. "Unless the old one turns up by tomorrow."

"O.K., team," Coach Peterson called. "Get out in the field for practice." He had just put the cardboard base in place.

Practice went fine that morning, and on the next morning too. But the stolen base still had not turned up.

After practice Coach Peterson called the team together. "Tomorrow is the big game," he said. "If we win that one, we're the Park Champs."

As the coach was talking, Mrs. Zervas appeared. She was carrying a big paper bag. She walked over to the coach. "I have a present for the team," she said. She handed the bag to the coach.

Coach Peterson looked surprised. "Why, thank you, Mrs. Zervas," he said. "What is it?"

"Open the bag, Coach," said Liz. "Then we can all find out."

"Well, I'll be," said Coach Peterson. He pulled a base from the bag.

"A new base," said Dave. "How did you know our base had been stolen, Mrs. Zervas?"

Mrs. Zervas laughed. "Because I'm the one who stole it. This isn't a new base. It's your old one. After Mark's accident I decided it needed fixing. Those little rips all over it were dangerous."

"You know what, Mrs. Zervas?" Mark said. "You're the best base stealer this team ever had."

On the day of the big game the stands were filled. The Lions took practice first. Then the Tigers had their turn. Mark was playing. His ankle was fine.

There was no score for three innings. Then the Lions pushed a run across. They scored another in the next inning. Then the Tigers tied it up. It was still tied at the bottom of the last inning.

"This is almost like the game with the Robins on Tuesday," said Liz.

"And Mark's at bat again," said Dave. "But this time there's no one on base. Too bad."

Mark swung at the first pitch. He hit a low liner over the head of the first baseman. He ended up with a single. Mark heard the fans shouting. "Come on, Tigers!" "Good work, Mark!"

On the first pitch to the next batter Mark took off for second. His timing was just right. He made it to second just before the catcher's throw.

"Safe," the base umpire called.

"That a boy, Mark!" Dave shouted. "Show them!"

On the next pitch the batter popped to the pitcher. Then Dave made the second out. He hit a fly to right.

I have to score, Mark thought. We have to win this game.

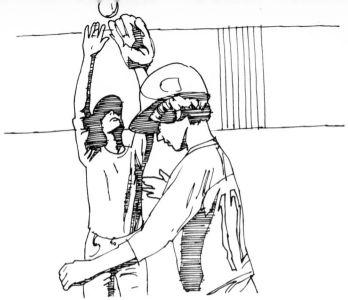

The pitcher let go of the ball on his second pitch. Mark took off for third. He beat the catcher's throw again. He was safe on third. But the throw was high! The third baseman jumped. But the ball was over his glove. It sailed out into left field.

Mark scrambled to his feet. He heard Mrs. Zervas shouting. "Go, Mark, go!"

Mark ran for home plate. The left fielder was scrambling after the ball. Mark crossed the plate with the winning run. The throw from left was too late to catch him.

The Tigers pounded him on the back. The fans raced down from the stands. Everyone was shouting. "We won!" "We won!"

"That was really something, Mark," said Mrs. Zervas. "I'll have to pass on my title as base stealing champ to you!"

Mark laughed. "We can share it, Mrs. Zervas," he said. "After all, if you hadn't fixed second, I might not have made it to third!"

"Three cheers for Mark and Mrs. Zervas," Liz shouted. And the whole Tiger team cheered.